T0193876

STAR BATTLES

The Valkyrie Saga

Book 1
Rise of the Ascendancy

Kenneth Michael Hamblett

Order this book online at www.trafford.com
or email orders@trafford.com

Most Trafford titles are also available at major online book retailers.

Printed in the United States of America.

ISBN: 978-1-4669-6070-1 (sc)
ISBN: 978-1-4669-6071-8 (e)

Trafford rev. 09/24/2012

 www.trafford.com

North America & international
toll-free: 1 888 232 4444 (USA & Canada)
phone: 250 383 6864 ♦ fax: 812 355 4082

INTRODUCTION AND THANKS:

I would like to thank all of my friends and family who always encouraged me in my writing and art projects with their constant encouragements. Above all else, I would like to thank God and Jesus Christ for all blessings bestowed upon me and for giving me creative talent. Thank you to my best friends Karen, Mike and my fellow military veteran and "wing man" James King. Finally, I would like to give a big thanks and "HOOAH!" to all my brothers and sisters in arms and uniform. Without our sacrifice that we give to our country, our freedom and liberty would just be science fiction. God bless you all!!!!

DEDICATION

I dedicate this book to my godfather, Deacon John Coussirat. He did many wonderful things during his lifetime and helped many people. May God bless his soul, and may he also bless his grieving wife, my godmother Loretta.

Secondly, I also dedicate this book to my beautiful and wonderful fiance' Elizabeth. She is my soul mate, and queen of my heart. I have many years ago given her the key to my heart.

A small dedication to all the USA military veterans young and old:

Kenny: An American soldier

Written by: Kenneth Michael Hamblett

Verse-1:

Let me tell you a story about an American soldier named Kenny.
He came home and got a letter in the mail, says, "go to war or go to jail."
When Kenny arrived at boot camp, he was met by pillars of fire.
This would change his life forever.

He sat in the barber's chair, turned around he had no hair.
He used to eat at McD's, now he eats MRE's.
He used to date a beauty queen, now he has his M-16.
He used to drive a Cadillac, now he's humping on his back.
With bullets flying over his head, he prays to God before going to bed.
Eight weeks later, Kenny graduates from boot camp with pride in his heart,
he even once again got to see his sweetheart.

First Chorus/Refrain:

Oh momma, momma can't you see, what the Army's done for him?
Oh momma, momma can't you see, what the Army's done for him?

Verse-2:

Kenny's warrior spirit has now been forged.
He's a lean, mean, fighting machine.
He heard his nation's call, he'd rather die than to let his nation fall.

Kenny got his marching orders and boarded a C-130.

Mission: Top Secret, Destination: Unknown, he never knows if he's ever going home. With his adrenaline pumping, at his drop zone he goes to jumping.

If his chute shall fail him, he has a reserve at his side.

If that reserve should fail him too, look out ground cause' he's coming through.

Tell his mom he did his best, bury him in the leaning-rest, with all his medals on his chest.

America the beautiful, all soldiers and veterans give their honor, allegiance, and victory to you.

Second Chorus/Refrain:

He's Kenny, a hard-core, Airborne Chemical Ranger, ready to face any danger.

Oh momma, momma can't you see, what the Army's done for him?

Oh momma, momma can't you see, what the Army's done for him?

I dedicate this to all those who have proudly served America in the Armed Forces both past and present. We must never forget the sacrifices and blood that has been shed by all our nation's veterans. May God bless you all.

FOREWORD

In the beginning . . .

The universe was without form. It was a cold, dark, black void. Billions of years ago, God creates the stars and nebular matter with his words, causing the "Great Bang." The universe then begins to form and take shape. Billions of galaxies are formed, containing the stars and other stellar material within it.

Several millions of years ago . . .

There was a beautiful world, home to the hunter-gatherer indigenous species called the Zendi.

The Zendi homeworld was home to many different types of civilizations. Some Zendi were nomadic, some were members of tribes. As time passed on, some of these tribes grew into vast city-states.

One cloudless night in the western hemisphere of the planet, a Zendi family of peaceful farmers were suddenly startled. They heard loud screeching noises from the night sky. They came out of their house with excitement and pointed to the twinkling stars. This family saw many explosions in the night sky, including tonnes of debris raining down through the atmosphere. Unknown to the people of this world, an immense space battle was going on in their home star system. Two warring alien civilizations, known as the precursors, were at each others' throats, each vying for control and supremacy of the stars. The two alien precursor species at the battle are the Aren and the Slavnians.

After everything became calm, the Zendi family went to go investigate the tonnes of debris that had rained down upon their land. The family was astonished that despite all the damaged debris, some of the advanced alien technology remained intact. The Patriarch of the family saw a gray-colored phallic shaped device with shiny colored buttons on it. He, in his curiosity was very cautious as to what the device might be. He decided to take a chance and slowly approached the device. When he was inches away, he bent down and retrieved the device.

He had absolutely no idea what it might be. One of the buttons was shinning a bright red light. He decided to take another risk. He aimed the phallic device at a charred bulkhead of the remains of the alien starship. He then pressed the button. Instantly, a red beam of light escaped from the device and hit against the derelict alien starship's bulkhead, which just as quickly and violently exploded and instantly vaporized the bulkhead while the remaining ashes fell onto the deck. The family's patriarch was amazed at what had happened. He realized he had found some sort of alien weapon. He wondered what other treasures he might find among the other mounds of debris.

He heard a loud whining noise. He went out of the derelict starship and saw a few feet away in a mound of debris, a bright yellow glow emanating from it. He again slowly and cautiously approached the next item. Moments later, he was a foot away from the glowing object. He squatted down and dug through the dirt and debris. A couple minutes later, he finally found what he was looking for.

He grabbed the black and gray-colored, square-shaped object and looked it over. It was closed but he could see the yellow glowing light creeping out of the crack in the front of the object. The object started to make quick soft beeps. After seeing that centimeters underneath the front crack of the device, there appeared to be a centimeter wide, four inch long slot in the front of the object. A small red-colored round object, slowly slid down the mound, falling onto his foot. He picked that up as well. He then decided to insert the red rounded object into the small slot. A few loud beeping noises could be heard. Suddenly, the object's top raised up, and the bright yellow glow turned soft blue and dimmer. On the inside bottom of the object were several different colored buttons and blinking lights. There was a predominately large oval shaped green button in the far right-hand corner. He decided to press it.

Suddenly an image of a person appeared onscreen, talking in a language he never heard before, while seeing strange alien script scroll to the left slowly. Then, a compartment door on the left hand side opened up. There were many other brightly colored rounded objects just like the red one found inside. The patriarch played around with all the other buttons of the device. Suddenly the image onscreen disappeared, replaced by that soft blue dim glowing light. He looked inside the opened compartment. He decided whether to insert the green colored round thing, or the blue one. He chose the blue.

He inserted the blue round object into the small disk slot after the red one ejected itself out of the slot. Instantly, other images and sounds could be heard from the view screen. The patriarch was again amazed at what all he saw onscreen. An hour later, he finally realized what he had found on his farmland. He realized he had found a plethora of alien advanced technology and instructions. He realized from this day forward, that his poor and struggling family will suffer no longer. That what he had found, was the key of usurping the power of the evil tyrannical king of his nearby city-state that annexed his farm into their sphere of influence. He realized soon, HE would become king and his family will have an abundance of wealth and power. He thanked the gods for his great find. They ruled but one planet. Over the next few ages, their influence would increase significantly and later grew into a mighty interstellar empire.

The patriarch didn't know he had helped his race to begin a new era for its civilization. He also didn't know, that his family's descendants would, with the help of the alien technology, to unite all the tribes and city-states into one planetary government, and that his family would remain as the next royal family in a new dynasty. He also wouldn't realize that after centuries after his death, his descendants would use this alien technology and improved on it to expand Zendi influence upon the universe.

Centuries later, the Zendi Golden-Age would begin, and Zendi civilization continued to prosper.This would be the beginning of a long and glorious time period in Zendi history. Centuries later, their interstellar empire would encompass the whole entire Milkyway Galaxy. The Zendi Emperor wanted to expand his empire outside of the galaxy, and spread Zendi influence upon other several nearby galaxies. Two centuries later, Zendi star portal technology was tried and became a success! The Zendi realized that they no longer needed to rely on there stardrive systems alone to travel vast distances, they had these spectacular star portals to help. These star portals were constructed in planetary orbits, smaller versions constructed planet side, and even star portals constructed in open space. The Zendi even constructed large outposts strung throughout the galaxies along with more star portals. A Zendi task force even made it to the nearest galaxy, the Andromeda galaxy. There, they continued to expand their power and influence. The Zendi Golden Age was the greatest time in the history of Zendi civilization.

This Golden age continued for many millenniums, that is, until the Great Revolt. Dozens and dozens of alien species, subjugated under Zendi rule tired of the shackles their Zendi masters put upon them. Dozens of these subjugated alien species rose up and entered into a great alliance with the thought of its main goal . . . freedom and liberty. This great revolt lasted for many centuries. The "darktimes", as the Zendi put it, has now begun. The insurrectionists took no mercy when confronting Zendi forces. Even Zendi civilians were hunted down and slaughtered gruesomely.

The Zendi now wishes that simple poor farmer, the Patriarch of the new Zendi era had never found that object on his farmland many thousands of years ago. The object he had found, the "Kohmra", it was realized, was the cause of the near total destruction of Zendi civilization. Centuries later, the great Zendi Empire fell into oblivion. Only a couple thousand Zendi remained alive. The rebels celebrated their great victory. They continued to bombard the Zendi homeworld, leaving few survivors, which would be forced to leave the cradle of their civilization behind, the few that remained scattered all over the known universe, always in fear of their former slaves, which continued to hunt them down. A whole culture and lanquage dies along with their crumbled civilization. Whatever really happened to the remnants of Zendi civilization remains a mystery.

Zendi influence will remain felt throughout the known universe, to be felt throughout the ages to come . . .

In the Twentieth Century AD

It is Earth year 1923AD, five years after the Armistice that ended Earth's "Great War"(WW-I). The German people are forced by the Allied powers to accept full responsibility for the war and pay reparations for all the damages caused by the war. Germany's infrastructure and economy was in ruins.

Together with many of his Nazi SA Stormtroopers, Adolf Hitler makes an attempt to take over the Bavarian State government. His forces are defeated by the German Army, and he is arrested by the authorities. Adolf Hitler is tried in court and found guilty of treason. He is then sentenced to serve several years in Landsburg Prison.

During this time, he began writing his two volume book entitled "Mein Kampf"(My Struggle). He also began to have visions in his sleep, visions of an Aryan empire that not only spans the globe, but a thousand year reich that spans the galaxy, dominated by the "master race." In 1924AD, he would get released from prison by the authorities after serving just a few months in prison.

It is Earth year 1932AD. The Great Economic Depression is destroying the lives of all humanity to deplorable levels. In Germany, conditions are even worst. For example, inflation is at an all time high, and it takes at least a thousand German marks just to buy a loaf of bread. More turmoil was ensuing, and the feeble aging President von Hindenburg, veteran of the past war, is president of the German Weimar Republic.

In the forests of Germany . . .

Adolf Hitler, Ernst Rohm, Heinrich Himmler, and several Nazi stormtroopers were at the clearing. Hitler's best friend Ernst Rohm asked Hitler what was going on. Hitler tells them all that a great big surprise for the German people will be arriving soon.

Adolf Hitler looks at his watch. He then looks up into the blue sky. He then sees a shiny point of light appear up in the sky, Hitler points to it. Then, in a matter of seconds, the shiny point of light drops straight down to the ground, and reveals itself to be a saucer shaped craft. Hitler has a big grin on his face.

The hatch of the strange craft opens up and the Nazis see a bi-pedal humanoid being walk down the gangplank. The being walks straight up to Hitler and gives a salute similar to the ancient Roman salute. Hitler responds by raising his right arm straight into the air at an angle, the fingers of his hand placed together. The strange being speaks, "Adolf Hitler, I am Commander Zorg of the Xendu Imperium. We are from the nearest galaxy to your own. We have a lot to discuss."

It is Earth year 1933AD. Adolf Hitler is elected as Chancellor of Germany. Later, the aging President von Hindenburg passes away. Adolf Hitler combines the powers of chancellor with that of President, naming himself the Furher(the Leader). The Reichstag passes the Enabling Act, giving Hitler unlimited authoritarian powers. The weak Wiemar Republic is now replaced by the grim Third Reich of Greater Germany. Many in Germany was happy and begun to celebrate.

. . . in the Twenty First Century AD

It is a time of great peril. The Earth is at war . . . again. The current date is April 4,2063AD at 2000 hours. Radio transmissions can be heard, "*Whiskey42, this is Foxtrot12 over.*"
"*Foxtrot12,roger. Awaiting the word.*"

The nite sky is pitch black, the clouds above obscuring the moonlite. The landscape is riddled with devastation. Lieutenant Reginald Noble, one of many army officers of the Eastern United States of America looks at the horizon with his nite vision goggles. A sergeant runs up to him and speaks, "Lieutenant, Division Commander Brigadier General Prescott is awaiting word from you if you and your troops are ready for advancement into the Russian capital."

Lieutenant Noble can see Moscow just over the horizon. He takes the goggles of and nods his head at the sergeant. He clears his throat. The sergeant speaks once more, "Sir, the General says our next offensive will begin with your word." Moscow, the last jewel of the European Hegemony is on the verge of surrender to the surrounding allied forces. Its major ally, the Eastern Coalition has already surrendered to allied forces months ago.

The war has been long and hard, with at least 5 billion people dead. The European Union was overthrown decades ago by Hegemony forces. From that point on, the European Hegemony had been pressing hard against NATO forces. Hegemony troops can be seen amassing along the front lines. The Lieutenant speaks, "Very well, the word is given."

"Yes,Lieutenant." The sergeant speaks into his radio, while the Lieutenant turns his head to address his troops.
"Hell Raisers, let's raise some Hell!"

The date is April 12,2063AD. The Battle of Moscow lasted for eight days. It is now 1430 hours. We see a bird's eye view of the devastated city. Then the scene changes onto Red Square. Commanders of both sides are there, the war has ended.

. . . in the Twenty Third Century AD

It is Earthdate March 2, 2202AD. The scene is on board the main bridge of the Terran starship *USS Thunder child* Zeus Class-Heavy

Cruiser, Captain Rachel Goddard commanding. They are in orbit around the colony world of Marcus-II. Nearby hangs a huge ancient alien artificial structure.

The science officer scans the object then speaks. "Captain, we have discovered another ancient Zendi Star Portal. Ma'am, I'm reading that the structure is feeding coordinates of a new phase lane.

"Well ladies and gentlemen, looks like we need to be brave and seek out yet more new civilizations. Keep our originating phase coordinates ready in case we need to jump back here in a hurry. I ask from all of you to trust me, as I've trusted you. We've done this twice before. You are a remarkable crew, the best crew I've ever served with. What say you?" says Captain Goddard. The whole bridge crew in unison reports that they are all ready to explore new civilizations. "Science officer Bartley, feed the new phase coordinates into the star portal and open the vortex."

"Yes, Ma'am, right away." The science officer manipulates her console. On screen, white lights from the structure flashes, until a large blue vortex opens up in the hollow middle area of the ancient structure. The helmsman reports that he's ready to make a phase jump into the new phase lane."

"Cross your fingers ladies and gentlemen . . . engage!," says the captain as she points to the main viewing screen. The starship enters into the rift then lurches starboard into a brand new phase lane. Fifteen minutes later, a blue vortex opens in front of them. The starship hurls itself through the vortex and out of a star portal.

A few seconds later the Captain orders for the ship to stop. The Captain speaks," Science Officer, full scan. Navigator, where are we?"

"Captain!," says the navigator," we have arrived 70,000 light years acrooss the galaxy! We are now on the other side of the galaxy."

The Captain stands up from her chair and she speaks. "My God! That would take us nearly a century to get back home using just our hyperdrive alone! Thank God the ancient Zendi star portals are still active."

"Captain," says the science officer, "I have scanned the star system. It is a binary star system, however, the closer yellow star and it's planets are nearly identical to your home star system. Indeed Captain, the third planet has nearly the same continental arrangement as Earth has, including the same nitrogen/oxygen composition."

"On screen," orders the captain. In two seconds they see the wondrous site, however several alien starships are on an intercept course to the *U.S.S. Thunder Child.*

The alien starships get closer, a beep could be heard. "Captain, we are being hailed," says the communications officer.

"On screen." A second later, the image of the alien can be seen. The alien commander stands up from his chair. Captain Goddard was pleasantly surprised. The alien commander is tall and slender, Caucasian skinned with pointy ears. She realized that the alien commander looks like creatures of Earth mythology called elves. She saw that the alien commander's crew was just as racially divers as her own.

The alien commander speaks," Greetings, I am Captain Sulvak of the Niconian Systems Commonwealth starship *Xal-One.* Welcome to our home star system. Your starship configuration is not in our database."

"I am Captain Goddard of the United Galactic Union starship *U.SS. Thunder Child.* We come in peace. Our universal translater picked up your language well, because it's similar to our home world's French language. I promise you Captain, we will not start any trouble in your neighborhood."

"Captain Goddard, I see that a lasting friendship between our two governments will last a long time. It is an honor to meet you. We are a race of psycho and telekinetic telepaths. We know your intentions are honorable. Let us send diplomats to sign a friendship treaty."

The present day . . .

PART ONE

ACT-I
Teaser/Prologue

SCENE-ONE

. . . in the Twenty Seventh Century AD

All was well in the Terran Star Empire. The sweeping reforms had long since been completed, a new constitution signed and ratified, the citizens of the empire were very happy and content with the current Imperial government. By this time, the brutal and tyrannical Jones Dynasty has long since been overthrown, replaced by the honorable Jenkins Dynasty, paving the way to a much more flourishing empire, ever since its citizens were given a voice once again.

Around two hundred years has passed since the start of the great reforms, and the empire's borders have expanded due to peaceful space exploration, and admitting new members into the empire. The infrastructure and military of the empire has been strengthened and the economy was booming. Most everybody was happy and supportive of the current emperor, and the Imperial Family.

The year is, using the Earth calendar, March 12,2607AD. The current Emperor is his excellency Wayne Richard Jenkins(now thirty five Human years old), alongside his loving and devoted wife, Queen Elizabeth Edna Jenkins(now thirty one years old). The royal children are Crown Princess Elizabeth Dana Jenkins(now thirteen Human years old), and her younger sister, Princess Rachel Marie Jenkins(now eight Human years old).

Most citizens in the empire adores the Imperial Family. However, there are a few citizens who do not love the beloved Jenkins Dynasty. There are those who have been plotting against the current regime, dreaming of returning the empire to a totally authoritarian society, believing in devouring the many civilizations in the galaxy. At least ten years ago, the Noble House McKinney had begun planting propaganda, preaching how House Jenkins, to House McKinney, had sold the Human race out to the "alien trash of the galaxy," as quoted from Duke Edward McKinney. Soon afterwords, a small xenophobic underground movement was established, called the Terran Storm Front. Ever since then, the House McKinney-House Jenkins feud became full blown in status.

Some citizens are worried that another civil war may erupt, but Imperial authorities have now reassured the citizens of the galaxy, that the Terran Storm Front is just a very small, fledgling organization with little to no influence in Imperial Society. As of now, Terran Storm Front operates in many semi-autonomous cells. Agents of the Imperial Intelligence Agency have been trying to locate and infiltrate these cells.

In the Antilles Sector of the empire . . .

Aboard the Imperial Starship *Red Lion*, Captain Andrew Davidson sat in his command chair, gazing at the main viewing screen on his ship's bridge. Long range scans detected an ancient Zendi outpost in this previously barely mapped sector of space. On the view screen, the ancient outpost is dangling in space. One hour earlier, the boarding party boarded the derelict space station. The Captain was amazed at the fact, that upon arrival in orbit of the old alien outpost, that the condition of the outpost was excellent, and that life support systems were still functioning. Upon additional scans, it was reported that the old outpost was safe enough to board.

The Captain was a handsome middle-aged Human with a short brown beard with a short hair style, neatly combed and parted on the right side. He took his right hand and smoothed his beard. He stood up and tugged down the bottom of his uniform tunic. He wondered what treasures, if any, that the boarding team have found already.

In the Earth year April 3,2609AD, Prince Kevin Michael Jenkins is born. All in the empire celebrates. Human telepaths tell the Imperial

Family, that the new born prince is wonderful and destined for greatness. The telepaths say that in a few decades time, a big galactic "storm" would occur. The new born prince and few other key people will help calm this "storm."

When Kevin was four years old, he would meet four year old Michael Manton. The Manton family is a house of nobility, and the prince and Michael would begin a lifelong friendship. It is said by the telepaths, that both children will bring glory to the empire decades from now.

Many years later . . .

In the year 2625AD, Prince Hamblett graduates from high school at the age of 18. By now, he's highly decorated in the empire's youth movement. The Imperial Family and the Manton Family are now allies by this time. Both families have a big graduation party at the Imperial Palace in Imperial City(was Washington,D.C.) on Earth. The prince's best friend Michael, has been accepted into the Imperial Military Academy, located in Annapolis,Maryland. Meanwhile, the prince has joined the empire's Marine Corps. He will ship out to basic combat training in just a few weeks.

Soon after a couple years, the prince quickly rises through the first 3 enlisted pay grades. Because of his hard work and dedication and deep devotion to the Marine Corps mission to the empire, he was quickly promoted to the rank of Lance Corporal. Prince Hamblett is a good soldier.

It is now Earth year 2629AD.It has been twenty years since a non-aggression pact has been signed between the Terran Star Empire and the Kreelag Imperium. An intense cold war had ensued ever since then, bringing the two empires on the brink of total war several times. The Kreelag is always hungry to pillage there neighbors if they can get away with it. Despite all this, the Terran Diplomatic Corps is ever resilient in solving things peacefully. However, in the past five years, things has gotten very intense between the two parties, including with the Kreelag

Emperor's knowledge of Terran sympathies towards a group of Kreelag revolutionaries, called simply the Kohnree, who are bent on overthrowing the Emperor, and usher in democratic reforms in a new Kreelag Democratic Republic that the revolutionaries wish to establish . . .

It's a beautiful afternoon in the Kreelag capital city on their homeworld of Kreelag-III. Serghompt Gum'tarph, an Imperial Guard is on duty, guarding the entrance to the Kreelag Royal Palace. Like all Kreelag, he has, under his forehead skin, attached to his skull, is a v-shaped bone running up from his nose with each arm of the "v" arching upwards above each bushy eyebrow to the top of his skull. On the top of his skull, four-inch horns protrude from the middle-top region of his skull.

Kreelag physiology includes slitted dark pupils with bright yellow irises, and they have long-sharp canines in their mouths. Their tongues are all naturally purple and long. The average Kreelag is tall and muscular. They usually have no facial hair except for the bushy eyebrows. They also have tan or brown skin. They have beautiful and lush jet-black hair on their head, usually grown long and then tied back into a "warrior's ponytail."

However, in the case of Gum'tarf, he's balding with short-cropped hair around the sides and back of his skull. He also has a short goatee that has grown on his face. He's wearing the traditional uniform of a Kreelag Royal Guard, and he stands there holding the traditional spear of a Royal Guardsman. He also wears the amulet of the Guard, with the variant according to his rank. It's very warm, and several small beads of sweat begins to pour out of Gum'tarf's pores.

Then suddenly, Gum'tarf comes to attention, as Kreelag General K'htareg approaches him. The General speaks gruffly at the guard. "Out of the way! I have orders from the Emperor himself to meet with him." The nervous Serghompt gulps and asks the General for his authorization datacard. Gum'tarf looks at the General's uniform. The General is two feet taller than him, with a full head of hair, according to what the Kreelag consider to be the "norm." The General is wearing a red cape, indicative of his rank, being held up by two huge red, black-spiked shoulder pads with gold cords in front attached to both shoulder pads. He's also wearing the collar insignia and harness, also indicative of rank.

To complete the General's ensemble, is black knee-high boots, and a long sword in a sheath, attached at his left side on his belt. The General smiles sarcastically at the guard, showing his perfect set of teeth, long sharp canines and all. The General shows Gum'tarf his authorization datacard. The guardsman takes it and reads it. He then gives it back to the General, gulps once more, then speaks." You may proceed into the palace General." The General puts the datacard back into his utility box, also attached to his belt, but on the right side. Gum'tarf moves out of the way and opens the front entrance of the palace. The General laughs triumphantly, as he enters the palace and walks down the main hallway to the royal throne room, laughing as several guardsmen and military personnel come to attention as he walked past them.

By now Prince Kevin Jenkin's battalion has endured many skirmishes against Kreelag forces in the Border World's Region, which is located among the current borders between the empire, Kreelag Imperium, and Kreelag occupied Kraylorian Assembly. He's very successful at helping to win many military campaigns, that he receives a battlefield promotion to the lowest Non-Commissioned officer rank of Corporal. He was even awarded the Imperial War Cross, a rare honor to be bestowed upon a corporal.

Months later, the prince's battalion gets deployed to a former Kreelag subject world of Jintaka. The Jintakans are celebrating with glee at their new found freedom. The Jintakans are so thankful to their liberators, that the Jintakan provisional government has filed for membership into the Terran Star Empire.

The prince's battalion gets transferred to the forest moon of Jintaka to pull for guard duty at a prison complex on the moon. Several days later, the prince got word that his best friend, now Lieutenant Michael Manton will serve as one of the prison's duty shift supervisors. Prince Jenkins is excited to see his friend again. The prince gets a communication from Lt. Manton, that he just got engaged to a wonderful lady of nobility named Marie.

On March 2,2630AD, the prince's battalion is celebrating his 21st birthday. In the afternoon on his special day, the prince receives news about the assassination attempt on his father, his majesty Wayne Richard Jenkins, now forty five years old. Though the assassination attempt was a failure, the Emperor had a near fatal injury. The empire's medical authority has informed the prince, that his father is in a vegetated comatose state. In just a few short hours, the Emperor dies moments after being taken off life support. The Imperial Bureau of Investigation found that the leader of the assassins was none other than Sergeant Major Ralph McKinney.

House McKinney has had a rivalry with the empire's Imperial Family for at least two decades. This rivalry plus the many assassination attempts on the Imperial Family and other houses of nobility, House McKinney caused themselves to be in a state of discommendation. They are stripped of all titles and rights of nobility, giving their house a status similar to that of a common household. Imperial investigators found through continued interrogation of the assassins, that the galactic terrorist network, the Hy-Vree hired House McKinney in order to cause instability in the empire. Further investigation find that the Hy-Vree were hired by the Kreelag Royal Family. The Kreelag was hoping that their assassination attempt would work, because they wanted the Terran Star Empire to be ripe for conquest.

Shortly after the emperor's death, his wife Queen Elizabeth Edna Jenkins could no longer cope with her grief and became a very paranoid mess. In the end, this led to the Queen to become completely insane. Her eldest child, Crown Princess Elizabeth Dana Jenkins had her mother commited to an asylum. The empire's Council of Regents then called up the Arbiter of Succession. The Arbiter in just a few days, had the Crown Princess to become the next Empress of the Empire.

The House McKinney-House Jenkins feud has thickened. The unfortunate reality, is that Lance Corporal Katrina McKinney was assigned to the prince's battalion, though a different company within the same battalion. With the news of her family's discommendated status, two months later, she would attempt an assassination on the prince as he slept. The prince's platoon mates saved his life and put Katrina into custody. The prince wanted to kill Katrina for her cold, vile, and dishonorable actions in cold blood, but his platoon mates stopped him and held him back. They told him to let Imperial Justice prevail upon Katrina.

Within a few days, Imperial Constables of the empire's internal security forces arrived on the forest moon to take inmate Katrina McKinney into custody. Prison supervisor Lt. Manton hands over the custody transfer datapad to Constable Leyton. The garrisoned forces have a pleasant surprise. The Empress arrived on the moon for a visit to the heroes of the Battle of Jintaka. After two days, the Empress, constables, and inmate McKinney depart the moon to head back to Earth to try the inmate and sentence her to a proper punishment. When the empress' starship reached two sectors away from Earth, the ship blows up with all hands aboard killed, including inmate McKinney. Investigations find that the ship was planted with a time bomb by the terroristic scum, the Hy-Vree. It is learned that a bounty was put on the head of the empress by House McKinney. The inmates kinsmen shrugs their shoulders and say that Katrina was just an unfortunate casualty of the bloody feud between the houses.

On October 2nd of that same year, Crown Princess Rachel Marie Jenkins was coronated as the next empress, as the previous empress' husband had been gruesomely assassinated. She appoints her younger brother's(the prince) younger sister, Patti Marie Jenkins as one of her closest advisers. On January 22,2631AD, a cease-fire was declared by the two fighting empires, and the non-aggression pact was once again reaffirmed. Kreelag occupation forces withdrew from Kraylorian space.

A month later, Prince Jenkins' garrison duties comes to an end. The Kreelag cedes several star systems to the Terran Star Empire. Prince

Hamblett was now assigned to the colony world of Anjilon-II in the Anjilon Prime star system. On this paradise-like world, he met a young and very beautiful Hispanic noblewoman by the name of Carolina Gallo. She is a native of Earth's South American continent, specifically a Human nation-state called Colombia. Soon afterwords, the prince and Lady Gallo began to romantically date each other.

A year later, they become an engaged couples and married each other a month later in a royal wedding. In June 2,2632AD, the happy couple conceives their first child. On February 8,2633AD, their first child, Alyssa Maria Jenkins is born. On January 20,2634AD, the Empress decides to abdicate the Imperial throne. Two days later, Crown Prince Hamblett is coronated as the next emperor of the empire. His new wife, receives the title of Queen. On September 13, 2636AD, the emperor met a young midshipman by the name of Karen Johnson. During the midshipman's second year at the Academy, Karen becomes Princess Alyssa's godmother. During the midshipman's third year at the academy, she was wedded to both the Emperor and Queen of the Empire. This wedding becomes the empire's first royal triad polygamous marriage. Although the non-aggression pact had been reaffirmed, old wounds are hard to heal.

SCENE-TWO

Earthdate: May 25,2640AD 1230 hours

It is a beautiful and sunny day on Earth in the eastern coast of the North American continent. It's graduation day at the Imperial Military Academy in Annapolis, and a proud day in a midshipman's or cadet's life, when they become commissioned officers in the Imperial Armed Forces of the Terran Star Empire. Even the empire's Emperor Kevin Michael Jenkins is at the ceremony to wish all of the graduates luck with their new careers.

Many guests, visitors, and alien dignitaries have come to celebrate. Some of the flags, banners, and pennants represents the empire, the empire's military, and some of the individual alien races that make up as members of the empire and its allies. The crowd hushes when they hear the national anthem of the empire being played. All in the crowd stand up. After the anthem is played, the Imperial song "Hail to the Chief" begins to play. Everyone remains silent and respectful, as the Emperor walks into view onto the stage. He is flanked by a squad of Imperial Guardsmen and women. To the immediate right of the Emperor, is the very loyal Grand Admiral Xavier Noble, cousin to the Emperor. To the Emperor's left is Supreme Marshal Marcus Tiberius Chambers, the Chief of the Imperial Guard. Behind the Emperor is Queen Carolina Gallo, Queen of the Empire, native of Earth's South American continent.

In the crowd of cadets and midshipmen being honored is class valedictorian Karen Johnson. This is an especially proud day for Karen. She worked hard for her commission during her four years as a midshipman at the academy. Soon she would no longer be the Emperor's secret mistress, but soon to become the Emperor's second wife alongside Queen Gallo. She forecasts herself a quick rise in the ranks because, naturally the Emperor is the Commander-In-Chief, the Supreme Commander of the Empire's military forces. The Supreme Admiral, James Leland Smith greets the Emperor on stage and salutes him. The Emperor returns the salute. The Supreme Admiral is the Grand Admiral's direct assistant. The song ends and everyone is commanded to sit.

The Emperor stands at the podium, flanked by Grand Admiral Noble and Supreme Marshal Chambers. The Emperor greets everyone and makes his speech. Then after that, the Grand Admiral speaks. Then, several honored guests, dignitaries, and senators make their speeches as well. Afterwords, the Commandant of the Imperial Military Academy is called up to make his speech. Then the graduating class' student president makes his speech. The commandant stands back up and calls Midshipman Karen Johnson to the podium to make her speech. Karen rushes up to the stage then makes her speech. The commandant stands back up and speaks. "Midshipman Johnson, in recognition for graduating top of your class, I reward you the Imperial Military Academy Valedictorian Ribbon."

Karen stands there proudly with her chest out. The commandant then places the ribbon onto the left side of her uniform, centered just above her left breast, 1/8th inch above the senior cadet variant of the Badge of Military Honor. She then salutes him and he salutes back. She is then dismissed to rejoin her fellow cadets and midshipmen.

The academy's registrar stands up to the podium. The cadets and midshipmen all stand up and get into a single-field line. One by one they get onto the stage as their names are called to receive their degrees, graduation plaques, Imperial Military Academy Graduate Ribbons, and a personal handshake by the Emperor himself. After receiving their handshake, they salute the Emperor while he returns their salutes. After every cadet and midshipman had crossed the stage and returned to their seats, the emperor stands at the podium and speaks.

"Ladies and gentlemen, I give you the class of 40'." With that, all the cadets and midshipmen clap their hands and cheer, while the audience does the same. Then one of the empire's patriotic songs play in the background to the tune of "Dixie." Though this is a very happy day, after the graduation ceremony, Grand Admiral Noble is the bearer of bad news to the Emperor. He takes the Emperor to the side and tells him the bad news.

"Your majesty, Imperial Intelligence has received word that our neighbor, the alien Kreelag Imperium has begun their assault on our colonies on the border, and also begun to devastate several member worlds. Bordering starbases and outposts have been put on alert, several have been destroyed as their assigned capital ships and starfighters went on the defensive. So far, millions of citizens have been killed. I'm sure the Imperial Senate will have an emergency session. They may also decide to vote to go to war with the Kreelag."

"Thank you cousin for telling me this. A pity that these new officers might be thrust into a war soon into their careers. However, they have been trained well for this very situation. I have faith in my officers."

CHAPTER-1

SCENE-1

Earthdate: May 25,2640AD 1640 hours

Every senator and Congressmen are assembled in an emergency
session in the Main Imperial Senate Chambers of the
Praetorium(Capital Hill). There's a lot of chattering going on. At all of
the entrances and exits of the chamber are members of the Praetorian
Guard, dressed in their uniforms of blue tunics and black pants, while
members of the Imperial Guard wear similar uniforms, except their tunics
are crimson.

Seated in the command section of the chamber is the Emperor
himself. Seated to his right is the Grand Admiral with a grim look on his
face. Seated to the Emperor's left is Queen Gallo. At the main podium
stands the beautiful Supreme Chancellor of the Empire Darla O'Neal.
To her right is the Praetor of the Empire, who is the "Vice-President"
of the Imperial Senate, whom is the Supreme Chancellor's assistant for
legislative purposes. Seated to the left and right of the main podium is
the Proconsul, Vice-Proconsul, Imperial Senate appointed Consuls and
Tribunes. After a few more minutes of chatter, the Supreme Chancellor
takes her gavel, strikes her podium with it, and calls for order in the
chamber. The chattering fades away as all eyes are on her.

"This emergency session has been called to discuss what to do
about the recent attacks on our sovereign territory by the Kreelag, who
has obviously broken the non-aggression pact that they signed with our
empire nearly twenty years ago. Both sides of this issue will be allowed to

make their case either for or against war with the Kreelag Imperium. We shall start with Senator Hygrax-II of planet Hydraxion-II." After awhile all of the senators made their case for or against war. Then their was a sudden outburst from Senator X'in from the planet Chaka-III. She stands up to be recognized. Then she shakes her alien fist into the air as she speaks angrily.

"My homeworld was one of the first to be attacked by the evil, vile, dishonorable Kreelag. By Chakan customs and traditions, we have a right to declare a 'blood duel' with the Kreelag! I vote for war!" The Chakan are a warrior race, breed for combat and full of customs and traditions.

Senator Ch'rella of the Charada stands up and speaks, "I also vote for war. My homeworld was attacked too!" After a few more words of debate from the Imperial Senate the decision has arrived to the Supreme Chancellor . . . war. Now the Supreme Chancellor presents the Imperial Senate's vote for war to ask for the Emperor's veto of the vote, or his concurrence. The Emperor then thought long and hard about the consequences of either decision he may decide to make. After a few minutes of talking with his advisers, including the Grand Admiral, he has finally made his decision. The Terran Star Empire was now officially at war with the Kreelag Imperium.

CHAPTER-1

SCENE-2

Earthdate: May 25,2640AD 2000 hours

O ut in the courtyard of the Academy, everyone there was in their evening best. The graduation ball is well underway. There is a buffet of foods and drink from Earth and alien worlds. The band finishes the song they were playing. Then after two minutes of everyone talking, the Master of Ceremonies speak, "ladies and gentlemen, I present you with the Emperor."

The band then plays "Hail to the Chief." As the Emperor made his way, the people parted and bowed their heads as he went by as a sign of respect. The Emperor was flanked by his wife and his lover, who themselves were flanked by a squad of Imperial Guardsmen.

The band finishes playing "Hail to the Chief", and the Emperor is at the podium. He raises his hand, and all eyes are on him. Flanked to his right is Grand Admiral Xavier Noble. To his left stand Supreme Admiral James Leland Smith. As usual, Imperial Guardsmen and women are stationed on the stage, throughout the audience, and along the perimeter of the courtyard. He begins to make another speech.

"Thank you ladies and gentlemen for coming out on this beautiful, warm, star-filled night of honor and celebration. As you know, we are at war with the Kreelag, after they had broken the non-aggression pact they signed twenty years ago with them committing several acts of aggression and skirmishes. They have continued to cowardly attack us by either direct skirmishes along our borders, or indirectly by them hiring the galactic terrorist network, the Hy-Vree. We have no choice but to defend ourselves. Our diplomats had tried in vain to reason with them. In response to continued Kreelag aggression, our empire has been, for at least a few weeks now, have been giving aid to Kreelag revolutionaries who are aimed at toppling the Kreelag Imperial government, and replacing it into a new regime of a democratic republican nature. These revolutionaries, are the Kohmree. I'm hoping to end this war soon, and replace the Kreelag Emperor with the leader of the Kreelag revolutionaries. Then, and only then, will victory will finally be ours, and then we can then rest easy."

The audience roars with cheering and clapping. After one minute all is silent once more, as the Emperor speaks again," Victory will soon be at hand. A new era of glory for our people will be here. Then nobody in our empire will have to fear the Kreelag nor its formidable Armada ever again. Everyone, enjoy your evening."

The audience roars into cheering once more. Unknown to anyone else, Ensign Karen Johnson and Supreme Admiral Smith gives each other a very wicked and devious grin at each other for a few seconds. After awhile, the audience begin to dance as music is played once more.

CHAPTER-2

SCENE-1

Earthdate: May 26,2640AD 0930 hours

The scene is in the Throne Room(Oval Office) of the Imperial Palace on Earth. The Emperor is sitting at his desk, sipping on a mug of warm earl gray tea. A chime at his office doors could be heard, "Yes, come in," says the Emperor. The double doors swoosh open, and in comes the Grand Admiral." Ah, Xavier, how is it going today?"

The Grand Admiral presents the Emperor with a datapad while he sports a grim look on his face. "Well Kevin, forces belonging to the Kreelag Imperium have been making new rounds of massive preemptive strikes on our colonies and outposts along the border regions."

"Well," the Emperor continues to read the datapad. When he finished reading it, he sets it down then he looks into the Grand Admiral's eyes and speaks, "I was hoping to settle things with the Kreelag sooner than expected. It looks like we must ask our elvish Niconian allies from the Delta Quadrant for some help. My friend, they may go to war alongside us. I shall now communicate with the Empress of the Niconian Systems Commonwealth."

CHAPTER-2

SCENE-2

Earthdate: January 2,2641AD 0800 hours

The scene is in the private bed chamber of the Emperor, located in the Imperial Palace(White House). It's been about eight months since the start of the war with the Kreelag Imperium. Lieutenant J.G Karen Johnson lay asleep on the bed eight months pregnant. Queen Carolina Gallo lays next to her and speaks to her husband, "the war goes well Kevin, and we also now know the gender of the unborn baby. I hope our six year old daughter, Princess Alyssa will love her half-brother."

"I'm sure she will Carolina. She is very sweet natured. Her half-brother will be a glorious new addition to the Imperial Family. The war goes great for our people. Victory will soon be upon us. The Trellians have been great spies for the Empire. They are one of the most loyal of our servants."

"Any word from Starbase 1865? Isn't that the Headquarters of Admiral Brian Abbot?"

"Yes my love, and Admiral Abbot is recovering from his war wounds. His right forearm was severed in battle. He's one of the greatest war heroes. Though a major wound was inflicted on the Admiral, Operation: Overlord was a huge success!" Also, Operation: Juggernaut is in the works. It is proceeding as planned. Soon the "weapon", a.k.a. The Omega Torpedo Device will be unleashed upon the Kreelag homeworld, if the revolutionaries do not topple the current Imperial regime that's still in power. Soon, the Kreelag Emperor will wish he and his wife had never started this war in the first place."

Suddenly, Karen begins to awaken and opens her blue-green eyes, then starts to look deeply into the Emperor's eyes while stretching her pregnant body. She then rubs her eyes then looks into Carolina's eyes. The Emperor then gently gets up and gently rubs the belly of his pregnant mistress. They then look into each others' eyes and smile.

The Emperor then passes the fingers of his right hand through her long, thick blonde hair. She was dressed in a pink night gown and panties. The Emperor was dressed in black shorts, while Queen Gallo was dressed in silky turquoise bra and thong panties, hugging her curvy Hispanic model-looking body. The Emperor and Karen lock hands together, then he leans down and romantically kisses his pregnant mistress. After two minutes of kissing they stop and smile at each other. They then both smile at Carolina. Then, Carolina leans towards Karen and the two "wives" of the Emperor lock lips and passionately kiss each other and rubs each others' breasts gently. The Emperor then goes to the other side of the bed and starts to kiss Carolina's neck and caresses her right leg. All three kept this passionate love-making up for a couple more minutes then stopped as Karen stretched once more then spoke.

"Oh, was I asleep again?", Carolina smiles at Karen, kisses her on her forehead and rubs her belly.

"Oh, Karen, I felt the Prince kick!"

"Yes, he does that a lot doesn't he?" Then the Emperor speaks.

"I love you ladies very much!" He then kisses Carolina, then kisses Karen." Karen, how does it feel to be Mistress of the Empire?"

"It's amazing baby. When our child is of age, he shall ascend to the throne, that is, if Crown Princess Alyssa doesn't want the throne." The Emperor smiles.

"Yes honey, it's wonderful. The bloodline of the Jenkins Dynasty will continue. I'm sure our son will bring great glory for the Empire."

Karen speaks," Is Operation: Juggernaut still being developed at the Central High Command(the Pentagon)?"

"Yes Karen, it's proceeding as planned. When we launch the operation, are you sure you want to be part of this very dangerous assignment if we have to launch it years from now?"

"Yes Kevin. Not only do I want to bring glory for the Empire, I want to bring glory and honor to the Imperial Family. I shall be a strong warrior for the Empire. I want to crush the Kreelag Emperor's throat personally. Any enemy of yours, my dear Kevin, is an enemy of the state. Is the task fleet going to still be launched by Starbase 347?"

"Yes, Supreme Admiral Smith's personal base will be the best gathering point for the task fleet. Again, this is going to be a very dangerous mission. Not many people, I'm afraid, will make it back home."

Karen speaks," I understand that Smith's personal fleet will lead in the attack. Why?"

"I have utter confidence in my friend's leading ability and his unquestionable loyalty to me. I can't wait until he plants the flag of the Empire on the soil of the soon to be vanquished Kreelag homeworld. Imperial Intelligence have reported that the Kreelag revolutionaries have had some successes against their own Imperial government. I have a feeling, that we will be victorious!"

With that, the happy triad smile at each other and begin to make love to each other again.

PART ONE

ACT-II

CHAPTER-1

SCENE-1

Earthdate: February 6,2641AD 0800 hours

The scene is in the waiting room at the Walter Reed Army Hospital, North America. Planet Earth. While in the waiting room, several people both military and non-military are waiting anxiously for the Empire's new bundle of joy to be born. The Mistress of the Empire was in labor, about to give birth to the Empire's First Son. The double doors whooshed open and Minister of State Carrier, member of the Imperial Cabinet comes out into the waiting area wearing his blue minister's robe and black hooded cloak, all eyes are on him.

The Minister speaks," Congratulations to the Empire, the First Son is born!" Everyone cheers as the Grand Admiral steps up to the Minister and speaks.

"Hey Carl, have they thought of the name for the baby yet?"

"Yes Xavier, the name of the healthy young lad is Kevin Michael Jenkins-II."

"Hail to the Emperor and the Queen. I'm glad you and I are the child's official godfathers."

Minister Carrier looks at the Grand Admiral's embellished uniform, then looks back into the Grand Admiral's eyes. "Yes, it's a wonderful day for the Empire."

Then afterwords, Senator Daphne Twiggs jumps up from her seat, smooths out her white senatorial robe and speaks, "The Imperial Senate will be elated with the good news!" Then, Sioux Indian Senator Black Hawk responds in kind.

"Yes this is a glorious day for the Empire, for a possible new warrior is born." Soon afterwords the news of the child's birth reaches across the empire, including Starbase 347 near the border with the Kreelag Imperium.

CHAPTER-1

SCENE-2

Earthdate: April 3, 2641AD 1430 hours

A big fleet is assembled orbiting the Alpha Centauri star system. Roosevelt Station is in orbit around the Centauri homeworld. The Emperor's birthday celebration is going smoothly. All sorts of people are present, including member species of the empire and foreign dignitaries from allied galactic nation-states.

The facility is adorned with flags and banners representing all those at the party. Music is playing and some are dancing, while others are talking. Then the Mistress of Ceremonies hushes the audience and "Hail to the Chief" is played. After the song is played, the Emperor and many others of the Imperial contingent are on the stage. Mistress of Ceremonies, Centaurian Jennifer Krysopolis introduces the Emperor to the audience. The Emperor is flanked by the Queen and by Karen Johnson, proud new mother of the Empire's first son.

The crowd cheers for a minute, then hushes as the Emperor speaks, "Ladies and gentlemen, we have fought long and hard against Kreelag forces. Soon, victory will be upon us, "the crowd cheers," let us not forget the Massacre of Zaled-IV by Kreelag hands. The Zaledians shall be avenged, and the flag of our empire shall wave on the Kreelag homeworld! Victory or death!!" The crowd then cheers "victory or death" a few times then cheers. The Emperor speaks once more, "Everyone, enjoy the party."

CHAPTER-1

SCENE-3

On the Centauri homeworld in the Alpha Centauri star system, the Imperial contigent and many others are now in the Great Hall. The Centauri Queen, Alyna Anistapolis is sitting on her throne, while the Centauri governor is standing to the right of her. Though the Centauri are equal members of the Terran Star Empire, the Centauri homeworld and its colonies are ruled by a matriarchy. The Emperor and company are laughing, having a great time during the after party. The Emperor makes a toast, giving honor to the Centauri people.

Then a loud roar could be heard above the glass dome of the Great Hall. Everyone looks up and sees an Erathian shuttle. It begins to decend further towards the ground and lands just outside of the Great Hall.

The shuttle's hatch opens and out comes Princess Aria, flanked by six Erathian Royal Guards. She and the guards approach Emperor Jenkins. The Centauri ruling council, all women, part way for the new visitors. When the Erathian delegation reaches one foot away from the Emperor, they stop. The princess bows her head at the Centauri queen, who returns a head bow to the princess. She then bows her head towards the Emperor and offers her right hand to him. She wears the ring of the Erathian Royal Family. The Emperor kisses the Princess' hand then smiles at her.

The Emperor speaks, "Princess Aria, the Empire always appreciates all the help from our Erathian friends."

"You're very welcome your majesty. We welcome any help from the Empire. By the way, happy birthday."

"Thank you Princess."

"As you know, there are those in my species who wish to overthrow the monarchy of my star principality."

"Yes Princess, I think it's a shame that there are those whom your great family has wonderfully provided for, and they, the rebels are ungrateful brats towards your family. I know in my empire's history that has happened several times as well. When my family took over the empire, we promised great reforms to the empire, a promise my family has kept with great honor."

Then a look of anger came on the Emperor's face. Both Queen Gallo and Karen Johnson gasped at what they saw. The six Centauri amazonian guardsmen saw what was about to happen and was about to make there move, the captain of the guard beginning to withdraw her sword from its sheath. The perpetrator grabbed his dagger, a murderous look of bloodlust on his face, unsheathed his dagger and tried to murder Princess Aria in cold blooded murderous rage!

Emperor Jenkins quickly unsheathed his royal dagger and quickly plunged it into the gut of the traitorous guard, spilling a lot of blood. The perpetrator drops his dagger and gasps, as more of his blood begins to spill out. He then drops to the ground, gasping for air and his body starts to twitch for a few seconds then stops. The Centauri Amazonian Guard squad, the Empire's Imperial Guard squad with Imperial Guard Supreme Marshal Chambers rushing to the scene. Grand Admiral Noble also rushes to the Emperor's side with concern on his face and speaks," Princess, Emperor, are you two alright?"

Captain Zander of the Erathian Royal Guards rushes closer to the princess, shock on his face. The Princess speaks," Yes I am. I somehow knew Bathor was a part of the rebellion." She then turns to Captain Zander and speaks to him," Go tell the shuttle's pilot about this. Have him contact our royal flagship the *RES Imperial Condor*." The Princess nods her head towards the fresh new corps on the ground and speaks again," We shall make sure that Bathor's family is arrested and their minds sifted to see if they are in rebellion as well."

Captain Zander speaks," Yes my lady, I live to serve thee!" He then runs outside to the shuttle and talks to the pilot. Servants of the Centauri Queen drags away the corps of the traitorous Bathor for incineration(cremation) according to Erathian customs. Before they drag the corps away, the Emperor wipes the blood on his dagger onto the corps itself then placed it back into its sheath. As the corps is drug away, the Grand Admiral spits on the carcass. After a minute things go back to normal. Several Centauri males quickly arrive on the scene to clean up the mess, and then the after party continues.

CHAPTER-2

Scene-1

Earthdate: May 24,2645AD 1420 hours

Sector-312G Near the border of the Kreelag Impcrium

It has now been a little over five years since the start of the war. Starbase347 hangs in space with a small fleet of capital ships gathering as well as many starfighters and other craft flying about. The scene changes to the office of Supreme Admiral Smith. He's one of the key military personnel in charge of Operation:Juggernaut, which has been in development for the past five years.

The Supreme Admiral is seated at his desk wearing his standard duty service uniform(class-A variant) with ceremonial red cape, denoting him as a flag-grade commissioned officer with some of his military badges placed onto his white tunic. A nervous female enlisted crewman is in his office giving him her full report. She's young, about 5'2" tall with shoulder-length brown hair.

The Supreme Admiral speaks," Thank you Crewman Daniels. Take this datapad to your commanding officer aboard the *ISS Fireblade*." He hands her the datapad and she takes it with her left hand. She gulps and salutes him. He salutes back. She does an about face and leaves his office.

Yeoman Jamie Adams, one of the Supreme Admiral's Petty Officers was standing in front of his desk. She was an attractive tall woman with her brown hair up in a bun hairstyle. She was wearing the class-A variant of the standard duty service uniform tunic with standard length black optional duty skirt with nearly knee-length black standard duty boots. She was holding a datapad and speaks to the Supreme Admiral, "Sir, Baron Samuels from Nagasaki colony needs for you to authorize something by your signature." She hands him the datapad. The Supreme Admiral takes the datapad and reads it. He then takes a writing wand and signs the datapad.

He then gives the datapad back to the yeoman. She takes it and salutes him. He salutes back and the yeoman leaves his office. Seconds after the office door swishes shut, a beeping noise from behind the Supreme Admiral's desk could be heard. He smiles really evil like, which he knows what this means.

The Supreme Admiral speaks, "Computer, start lock out program Omega Mu."

"*Complying*", said the computer in a calm computerized male voice. A clicking sound could be heard from his office doors and a red-colored security field flicks over the door. The lights dims to a shade of blue and his office door locks. Also, an undetectable communications dampning field fires up, so starbase security personnel will not be able to monitor his communications.

The Supreme Admiral swivels his chair towards the back wall of his office. A monitor screen is on the back wall as well. He presses a blinking red button next to the monitor screen and seconds later, a dark figure can be seen onscreen. The dark figure is a Kreelag envoy, which starts to speak in the Kreelag language, "are we on a secured channel?"

The Supreme Admiral reply in Kreelag language," yes L'tan Zare. Not even my minions in the conspiracy can crack my codes."

"I have just received word that your son has celebrated his fourth birthday back in February at the Imperial Palace on Earth. Does you Emperor suspect anything?"

The Supreme Admiral laughs," No. Soon the Imperial Family will be dead and the Kreelag will rule over Earth, as long as your Emperor still promise to install me as the next leader of Earth."

"Of course! You will make a great Primarch of Earth. You have the gratitude of the Kreelag Imperium. Soon you will be wedded to Karen and your son will continue your bloodline. Emperor Jenkins will not know what happened until it's too late. Soon, the Terran Imperial Family will be assassinated and Kreelag influence will expand throughout both the Alpha and Beta Quadrants. My Emperor still promises to reward you and Karen for your loyalty. We shall proceed as planned. How about the 'weapon?' Is Captain Jonathan England still loyal to our cause?"

"Yes! He hates Emperor Jenkins with passion, and he's strictly loyal to me. The 'weapon' is being installed on his ship as we speak. Nothing will get in our way. Once we deploy the 'weapon', a new era will begin and the Jenkins Dynasty will end with no heir to the throne. A new dynasty will begin, and my family will rule the Earth, but will pay tribute to the glorious Kreelag Imperium. All member species in the Terran Star Empire shall become subject species and servants subserviant to the Kreelag. Not even the normally telepathic Niconians do not suspect what the conspiracy is going to do with their technology."

"Excellent! I shall make a full progress report to our Emperor. He will be most pleased with your progress."

"Hail to Emperor Z'uergla, his wife the Empress and to the Kreelag Imperium!" The screen goes blank and Supreme Admiral Smith swivels his chair forward and sports a big, evil smile on his face. Then he wickedly laughs," yes, Primarch Smith does have a nice ring to it."

The scene switches to outside of the starbase, orbiting planet Kalandra-III. A much bigger fleet is now in orbit with the task force's flagship, the ISS *Red Dragon* prominently present, Captain Jonathan England commanding. You can also see an ancient Zendi Star Portal in the distance.

-END OF PART ONE-

✦ ✧ ✦ ✧

PART TWO

ACT-I

CHAPTER-1

SCENE-1

Earthdate: July 20,2645AD 1840 hours

Earth-Imperial Palace(White House) throne room(Oval Office)

It's a pleasant evening with Emperor Jenkins and Niconian Star Commonwealth Empress Zana sitting down, both sipping on mugs of warm earl gray tea. Supreme Marshal Chambers is standing near Emperor Jenkins, wearing the crimson tunic and black pants of the Imperial Guard. Sitting next to the Emperor is his wife, Queen Carolina Gallo, who is wearing a silky light blue short-sleeve shirt with low neckline, black mini skirt while showing her midriff, and black high heeled close-toed shoes.

Empress Zana is sitting across from the Emperor and his wife. She has fair skin, blue eyes, and jet black long hair. She puts down her tea cup and puts a few strands that are over her left ear behind her left ear, revealing her elvish pointy ears. The Emperor always has felt that most elvish cultures are very beautiful and elegant. The Empress is wearing a purple gown that has a large key-hole, revealing her ample cleavage of her firm c-cup sized breasts. Her gown has two splits up in the sides, and she's wearing pink boots.

The Empress smiles then speaks," Emperor Jenkins, this tea of yours is good."

"I'm glad you like it. I myself have enjoyed the blue Tarkhaelian apples you've brought us from the Delta Quadrant."

"I see the war goes good for you."

"Yes Empress, and we can now finally end this horrible war with the advanced technology of the Niconian people. Tell me, was it easy bypassing your rebellious ascendic cousins based on planet Riconia?"

"Well Kevin, I had my best fleet transport myself and the 'weapon' to you from my homeworld of Niconia of the Delta Quadrant. The ancient Zendi star portals, our hyperdrives, and our stealth technologies also helped us. Actually, the 'weapon' is based on an ancient Zendi 'doomsday' weapon. We just improved on it. We have also installed deadly mauler ray cannons onto your command ship. I think it will now be evenly matched with the dreaded Kreelag Armada's Command Ship. The mauler rays will be able to destroy the smaller Kreelag Sentinal class-Escort ships, actually overkill them. Despite all that, many Niconians feel our people will be one again . . . someday."

"Yes, I hope the hatred between your people will end soon. A little over one thousand years of hatred is far too long and sorrowful."

"Kevin to that I drink."

Emperor Jenkins and Niconian Empress Zana both take their tea cups, clink them together gently and they both take a sip once more.

CHAPTER-1

SCENE-2

Earthdate: August 12,2645AD 1840 hours

Kreelag Imperium-Z'kahr Star System

A massive space battle is occuring. Massive explosions in space can be seen as Terran and allied starships of all kinds and sizes continue their offensive assault against Kreelag forces. The scene switches to the bridge of the Terran starship *ISS Yukon*, Commodore Jonathan Kim commanding. His communications officer, a female felinoid Massi named Mauvette speaks with a feline 'purring'-like voice," Sir, I have Admiral David Harding hailing us."

"Put him on screen."

"Aye, sir." The image of spacebattles is replaced by the image of the Admiral, a middle-aged caucasian Terran man with short brown hair(graying at the temples), and brown moustache. He speaks.

"Greetings Commodore."

"Hello Admiral."

"Your orders Commodore, is to lead Echo 82nd Task Wing towards the Kreelag outpost orbiting the planet and destroy it. Then, you may land your marines on the planet and liberate its native species. Understood?"

"Yes, sir."

"Good. Good luck Commodore. Admiral Harding out." The image of the Admiral is replaced by images of space battles once again.

"Lieutenant Mauvette, open a channel to all ships in our task wing."

"Channel open, sir."

"This is Commodore Kim, Echo 82nd Task Fleet commander. You all know the Admiral's orders . . . engage!" The scene then changes to space, the intense battle continues as Echo 82nd Task Wing heads towards the Kreelag outpost.

CHAPTER-2

SCENE-1

Earthdate: August 12,2645AD 1850 hours

The scene is on board the Command Operations Deck of the Kreelag outpost orbiting planet Z'kahr-III. A Kreelag Non-Commissioned Officer speaks," Prefect Z'tahn, Terran and allied forces are approaching us. Your orders, sir?"

Prefect Z'tahn has a smug, cocky, overconfident smile on his face. He speaks," You are to raise defensive shields, arm all laser and pulsar batteries and load all missile and torpedo tubes. Our new wraith torpedoes should devastate the pathetic wretches. Tell all fighter wings to be prepared to launch. So, the 'monkey boys' and their friends have come out to play? Launch all fighter wings. We must destroy all of their bombers!"

"Yes, Prefect. Giving launch orders immediately."

CHAPTER-2

SCENE-2

The scene changes to outside the alien outpost. All three of the outposts' fighter wings launches out of the main hanger deck, as its defensive shields are raised. The scene changes to the inside of the cockpit of a Terran starfighter. Its pilot, a Naturi speaks," Echo leader, do you see what I see?"

Commodore Kim's voice comes out of the cockpit's speakers," *Yes. Protect those bombers at all costs.*"

"Aye, sir. Victory or death!" A massive and very intense dog fight occurs. However, due to the skills and courage of Terran and allied forces, very few allied bombers were destroyed. One by one, Kreelag starfighters are destroyed with fewer loses for the allied forces.

Most allied bombers courageously heads towards their new objective, while others continue with destroying other areas of the outpost. The outpost then fires its new wraith torpedoes at a nearby allied capital ship. The two wraith torpedoes hit their mark, instantly vaporizing the capital ship. This surprises the allies. Now they have to work harder to destroy the outpost's torpedo tubes.

With a stroke of luck, the task wing all cheer, because reinforcements, the 73rd Task wing, have been assigned to assist the 82nd Task Wing in destroying this powerful enemy outpost with the word of new Kreelag wraith torpedo missile technology. The fresh new allied fighters and bombers begin to aide in the destruction of the mighty outpost. At this point in the battle, few intact Kreelag fighters remain. A few minutes later, the Kreelag outposts' wraith torpedo tube is destroyed, all allied forces cheer. The tube's explosion sets off one of the awaiting wraith torpedoes, causing a chain reaction, and leaving the outpost vulnerable. After awhile, the three Kreelag starfighter wings are severally devastated. Few Kreelag pilots successfully eject from their disabled fighters, only shortly to be picked up by allied patrols to become prisoners of war. With few enemy fighters left, the allied bombers begin making their bombing runs on the Kreelag out post, while remaining allied fighters try to take out the outposts torpedoes and missiles that are beginning to be fired at allied bombers. The outpost's mighty krulandrian armor is destroyed, leaving the outpost very vulnerable and "dead in the water."

CHAPTER-2

SCENE-3

Earthdate: August 12,2645AD 1920 hours

Operations Deck-Kreelag Outpost

"Prefect!," yells the Kreelag NCO," We have only two starfighters left, both layers of deflective shielding is gone, and hull integrity is down to 30%! Also, all laser and pulsar batteries are burnt, life support is failing! We barely have any armor left with only one missile tube barely intact! What will we do!"

The station shakes a few more times as more smoke begin to rise. The scene changes to view the Prefect, as all emotion fades from his face. He stands straight up. "We die."

The scene changes to the outside of the outpost, with allied forces continuing to fire on the outpost. Moments later, the outpost looses containment and explodes. The scene changes once more to the bridge of the Terran starship *ISS Yukon*. Cheers on the bridge and on all communications channels could be heard.

"Communications Officer, tell the launch decks of all our two task wing forces to launch all Marine landing craft and their fighter escorts."

"Aye,Commodore," says Lieutenant Mauvette in her usual purring voice."

CHAPTER-2

SCENE-4

Main Hanger Deck-*ISS Yukon*

A Marine Corps brigade is assembled in the hanger deck. They all have their tactical accessories on as well as some units with battle armor on. They are all at the position of parade rest. You can see other crew scurrying around the many craft in the hanger deck, prepping the Marine landing craft for launch as well as fueling squadrons of starfighters.

Before the assembled brigade of marine corps troopers and officers, stands the brigade commander Colonel Thaddius Powell. He speaks some words of encouragement. "Alright Helldogs, the Navy boys and girls have done their part, now it's time to do ours! Some of you may not make it out alive, but we will all, as a team, do our best to win the battle to sustain our freedom. I know we all refuse to become slaves under the tyranny of the dishonorable Kreelag. For freedom's and honor's sake, I ask that you do your best. No one quits! For our great leader of our empire, freedom and honor, Helldogs . . . MOUNT UP!!!! Brigade, attention! Move out!"

Every Marine trooper and officer in the brigade crisply goes to attention. They all yell out in unison, "HOOAH!!!!" Then the officers give all their troopers orders to board their designated marine landing craft.

CHAPTER-3

SCENE-1

Earthdate: September 6,2645AD 0200 hours

Kreelag Home Star System

The Kreelag is almost in defeat. The once great and feared Kreelag armada, as well as their orbital defense batteries are all but wiped out. The once arrogant and prideful Kreelag are now almost on the throws of begging the Allied forces for mercy.

More Kreelag space installations explode. The scene switches over to the bridge of the Terran Command Ship *ISS Red Dragon*, Supreme Admiral Smith's flagship. The starship is positioning itself in orbit of the planet. Captain England stands up. He paces in circles four times. He starts to sweat out of nervousness. He then touches a button on his command chair and speaks," Supreme Admiral, we are now in orbit around the Kreelag homeworld."

"Excellent! Any word from the Kohnree revolutionaries? Have they secured there new government in the Kreelag Royal First City?"

"None, my Lord."

"What a pity. The Kreelag revolutionaries knew they had all this time before the ultimatum was discussed. Well, the new Kreelag government will have to make due without their native homeworld. Captain, you know what you have to do now."

"Yes, my Lord."

"Make it so Captain."

"Yes, my Lord." Captain England presses the button once more. He looks around at his bridge crew. Several personnel nod their heads at him, with semi-nervous looks on their faces. "Prepare to deploy the 'Weapon'."

"Aye, sir. Now arming the Omega Torpedo now," said a Norovian tactical and weapons officer. A minute later a beep is heard from the tactical and weapons station. "Sir, Kreelag reinforcements are jumping out of hyperspace!" A minute more and other beeps are heard. "Sir, several additional Kreelag starships are coming out of stealth mode!"

"How did the Kreelag get stealth technology!?," said the ship's Executive officer, African-American Terran Commander Rodney Ellis-III in an excited tone of voice. This battle gets even dirtier eh? How many new Kreelag ships do you read?"

"I read fifty four that came out of hyperspace uncloaked, then the second group which came cloaked, sixty additional Kreelag starships, making it a total of one hundred and fourteen additional Kreelag starships joining the battle!"

Then beeps from the communications station can be heard. Then a voice comes through the speakers. "This is First Admiral Tal Ocet, of the Kreelag Revolutionary Kohnree. We are here to give assistance to our Terran friends. We shall now battle the fifty four Kreelag Imperial ships that came out of hyperspace before us. May the energies of Vadani be with us."

Commander Ellis smiles and says, "Well, I guess we don't have to use that horrible doomsday weapon after all."

Captain England speaks in a smug voice," I don't agree, Commander." The ship's commanding officer smiles then stands up from his command chair. He grabs his laser pistol from its holster and begins to jab it into the Commander's chest, surprising the muscle-bound Executive Officer and several others on the bridge. Some of the bridge crew gasps in disbelief, the nervous others, with evil grins on their faces.

Commander Ellis raises his hands up in surrender and speaks, "Captain, what is going on?" The ship's Second Officer(third in command) smiles and takes Commander Ellis' pistol and officer's dagger from the Commander's belt.

"Simple Commander. It's a coup de'etat."

The Commander states in a stunned voice, WHAT!?"

"That's right! Soon the 'weapon' will be turned over to the Kreelag Royal Authority. Also, the Imperial Family on Earth will be assassinated, and a new bloodline will rule over the empire!"

"Captain, no . . . this is treason!Why!?"

Captain England jabs his laser pistol once more at the Commander's chest. "A simple answer I'll give to you Commander . . . power, unlimited power. If our little conspiracy wins, I'll become the next Grand Admiral of the military forces under a new third dynasty. The Jenkins Dynasty will fall, and the Kreelag Royal Authority will continue to reward anyone loyal to them. The game is over now Commander, checkmate. We've aleady won. I shall now order for the 'weapon' to decimate those loyal to Emperor Jenkins. Security! Escort the Commander to the brig . . . and Commander, do enjoy doing a lifetime of hard labor at a Kreelag prison camp you pathetic wretch!" He then slaps the Commander's face with his free hand.

Suddenly, beeps can be heard from the tactical and weapons station. "Sir, the ancient Zendi Star Portal is activating!" The star portal flashes white light a few times, then a red-colored vortex is seen eminating from the portal. A few seconds later, Niconian starships can be seen jumping out and joining the battle.

Captain England rubs his chin for a few seconds then points at the view screen and asks," are those from the Niconian Systems Commonwealth, or from the Niconian Ascendancy headquartered on planet Riconia?"

After checking his readouts, the tactical and weapons officer gives a nervous look on his face and says," from the Commonwealth,sir!"

"Lieutenant, just how many Commonwealth capital ships are out there now?"

"Captain, I count two hundred and fifty new Commonwealth capital ships. They are now engaging forces loyal to the Kreelag Royal Authority!" After hearing that, Captain England's face turns white and a look of utter horror can be seen on his face.

By now two security officers loyal to the conspiracy holds Commander Ellis by his arms. Commander Ellis says with a big grin," Who's lost now, sir?" Captain England slaps the Commander once more in the face a spits towards his boots.

"Arm all mauler ray cannons as with all laser, pulsar batteries with the mass driver cannons. Employ the 'weapon', DESTROY THEM ALL!!!!," the Captain screams." Oh, and do kill Commander Ellis!"

Some beeps can be heard from the tactical and weapons station, its officer spoke frantically, "Can't sir. Our deflector shields suddenly went down and the Omega torpedo(the weapon) has been deactivated and encrypted by a lock out code of Niconian origin!" More beeps can be heard. "Sir! Niconian Commonwealth troops have docked into our ship and begun their siege!"

Captain England screams out, "all activated guns . . . FIRE!!!!"

"Captain, Niconian ships surround us on all sides, except in the front." Suddenly, a massive Niconian dreadnought decloaks in front of the *ISS Red Dragon*, firing laser and pulsar beams into the hull of the Terran ship, viciously shaking it. This shaking knocks Captain England off his feet, crashing him into a rear bridge station. That station's posted officer is loyal to Emperor Jenkins. The officer grabs the captain's skull, and thrusts the captain's face into the console, causing sparks and the captain's face to be partially burnt.

"I'll get you for this Ellis,personally!," gasps Captain England. Then the aft station's officer unsheathes his officer's dagger and quickly thrusts it into both of Captain England's eyes, making him scream in horror. Commander Ellis quickly gets himself up off of the bridge's floor. He quickly grabs the captain's laser pistol and shoots the second officer.

The bridge doors slide open and Niconian shock troops fill the bridge, arresting all members of the conspiracy. The head officer of the shock troops speaks, "Greetings friend of the Commonwealth. We are here to help."

Commander Ellis wipes sweat off of his brows and speaks," Thank you."

Then, an officer loyal to the Emperor speaks, "Commander, we are being hailed."

"On screen."

The image onscreen is replaced by the image of a Niconian starship commander. The elvish starship commander wore the gray and white uniform of the Niconian Royal Navy. His rank insignia displayed proudly on his left breast. He was tall with blonde hair(graying at the temples) with blonde goatee. He smiles and speaks," Hello friend. The "cavalry has arrived," as you Humans say.

Commander Ellis smiles and nods at the Niconian ship commander and speaks," We appreciate the assist Captain. On behalf of our Emperor, I thank you. My ship is split into two factions, but, thankfully, your troops are helping our security officers loyal to the Emperor regain control of the ship. Again, thank you."

"It's an honor to help the friends of our queen. Now, I think it's time to, as you Humans also say, 'to get back to work.' We shall provide cover fire for you." The image of the Niconian ship commander is now replaced by the space battle.

A beep could be heard on the main bridge. A loyalist tactical and weapons officer speaks, "Sir, main hanger crew is reporting the unauthorized launch of Lt. Commander Johnson's personal ship! The projected course is towards the Kreelag fleet!"

The small Antares class-starship can be seen flying away from the Terran flagship towards the Kreelag fleet. "Hail that ship!," Commander Ellis shouts as he points to the main viewing screen. The image of space battle is replaced by the cockpit of the fleeing Antares class ship's command crew. That crew is none other than Lt.Commander Karen Johnson and Supreme Admiral James Smith, both had evil smiles on their faces and Supreme Admiral Smith showed in his hand a small datachip.

"What's wrong Commander, shocked that I have a copy of the dataplans of the Omega Torpedo Or that you now have a civil war on your hands?" Beeps could be heard on the Terran flagship. Supreme Admiral Smith continues, "Ah, Commander, that beep should inform your tactical officer, that the civil war has begun. I shall become the new Emperor, and Karen shall become my queen." The Supreme Admiral laughs like a villain in triumph.

"Never! You two traitors will be hunted down and executed for this!," screams Commander Ellis.

"We shall see Commander, we shall see. You have now just witnessed the Rise of the Ascendancy. Your blood will paint the way to the future. The old glory days of the empire's future will return. *S.S. Valkyrie* out." The image is replaced by space battle. The battle rages on, and now dawns the Second Terran Galactic Civil War, as those Terran ships loyal to the Ascendent seperatists attacks loyalist forces, at the same time, Kreelag forces loyal to the Kreelag democratic movement, the Kohnree start attacking Imperial Kreelag ships and Terran separative forces.

Will this spill certain doom to humankind and pit the galaxy in a period of darkness, or will their be a new hope, soon to dawn on the battlefield? Deo Vindice.

-THE END-